"Now look," the farmer said. "That dog's dangerous. She's on my land, worrying my sheep. I don't want anybody getting hurt."

"We don't want Skye getting hurt," Emily said. "She hasn't done any harm."

"Hasn't done any harm?" the farmer repeated. "You don't know what you're talking about, young miss. That dog has just killed one of my sheep."

Emily gasped. Neil stared at the farmer.

"She wouldn't," he said, alarmed. "I don't believe it."

The farmer snorted. "Have you had a good look at her?" he asked.

Neil turned round and had a proper look at Skye for the first time since she came flying over the hill. She was no longer the beautifully groomed dog she had been earlier in the day. Her coat was tangled and, worst of all, there were flecks of blood round her muzzle and spattered over her ruff.

"Oh, Skye . . ." Emily's words were almost a sob.

Titles in the Puppy Patrol *series*

More Puppy Patrol stories follow soon

Puppy Patrol

Saving Skye

Jenny Dale

Illustrated by
Mick Reid

A Working Partners Book

MACMILLAN CHILDREN'S BOOKS

Special thanks to Cherith Baldry

First published 1998 by Macmillan Children's Books
a division of Macmillan Publishers Limited
25 Eccleston Place, London SW1W 9NF
and Basingstoke

Associated companies throughout the world

Created by Working Partners Limited
London W12 7QY

ISBN 0 330 35492 2

Copyright © Working Partners Limited 1998
Illustrations copyright © Mick Reid 1998

1 3 5 7 9 8 6 4 2

A CIP catalogue record for this book is available from
the British Library.

Typeset in Bookman Old Style
Printed and bound in Great Britain by Mackays of Chatham plc, Kent

Chapter One

Neil flinched as his sister, Emily, prodded him in the back. "Go on, then! What are you waiting for?" she said accusingly.

"Just don't rush me, OK?" Neil snapped back. He peered round the door of the vet's waiting room and breathed a huge sigh of relief. He had timed his entrance perfectly. Evening surgery had finished and nobody was waiting. Through the open surgery door he could hear Mike Turner and his nurse, Janice, packing up for the night.

At the sound of their voices, the vet came through into the waiting room, wiping his hands on a towel.

"Hello, Neil," he said cheerily. "Come in. What brings you here?"

Mike Turner regularly worked with Neil's parents, Bob and Carole Parker, who ran King Street Kennels just outside the small country town of Compton. Along with the boarding kennels, they also ran a rescue centre for abandoned, stray and ill-treated dogs. Neil loved to get involved in kennel affairs and had asked Mike's advice about some very strange canine problems in the past.

However, Neil had never approached Mike with a problem as strange as the one he had now. Reluctantly he stepped forward, tugging gently on a lead. A dog followed him into the room.

"You see," Neil said hesitantly, "it's like this . . ."

Mike Turner was wide-eyed with amazement. Janice, standing just behind him in the doorway, gave a little squeak and dropped a batch of record cards which scattered all over the floor. "What on earth have you got there?" asked Mike, incredulously.

Neil looked down at the dog. He was a mongrel, with floppy ears and rough, curly hair. He sat quietly at Neil's feet – bright-eyed, wet-nosed, panting happily as he sat by his master. Just a normal healthy dog – except that his wiry coat was a dazzling, eye-aching, incredible fluorescent pink.

"His name's Bundle," said Neil, his face reddening.

Mike clamped his lips together as he tried not to burst out laughing. "Bundle . . . yes. Hmm . . . I see."

"It's not funny!" Neil yelled. "*You* didn't have to bring him here! Do you know what it's like, walking a pink dog through the middle of Compton?"

Neil glared at the vet, who gave up his struggle and collapsed into gales of laughter.

"Sorry, Neil," Mike gasped. "I know it's not funny. But a pink dog? I don't often see psychedelic dogs in the surgery."

Neil knew this was no way to treat a dog, but he had never felt so ridiculous in his life. He looked down into Bundle's bright, whiskery, pink face, and gave up, joining in the laughter.

Emily looked at Mike and her brother with disgust. "Honestly!" She went over to Janice and helped to pick up the scattered record cards.

Still smiling, Mike Turner squatted in front
of Bundle. "He's a lovely chap, Neil. Come on,
Bundle, let's have a look at you." Mike
rumpled the dog's ears and Bundle thumped
his gaudy pink tail rhythmically on the floor.

Mike took Bundle's lead and led him into
the surgery. Neil and Emily followed, and
watched the vet lift the big hairy dog onto the
examination table.

"He's still young," Mike said. "I reckon he's

got a lot more growing to do. Look at these feet!" He picked up one of Bundle's paws. "If you want to know how big a dog will be when it's full-grown, always look at its feet. Bundle's are like dinner plates."

"Dad thought he might be part Great Dane," said Neil.

"I think he might be part horse!" Mike grinned and ran his hands expertly over Bundle. "Where did you get him?"

Neil took a deep breath. He ruffled his untidy brown hair and launched into the story. "Two students from Padsham Agricultural College brought him into the rescue centre. They told us he was a stray, hanging round the canteen and eating scraps out of the bins."

Mike raised his eyebrows. "That must have been a sight!"

"No, he wasn't pink then," corrected Neil. "That was for Rag Week. Some bright spark had the idea of dyeing him pink and sending him round with a collecting tin. It was all in the name of charity, apparently."

"But that doesn't make it right, does it?" said Emily, stonily.

Neil noticed that Mike had stopped smiling.

"Of all the stupid, irresponsible things to do! Did nobody think about how the dog would feel?"

"I think the boys who brought him in were sorry," Emily said. "But they weren't the ones who dyed him pink."

"And they haven't got anywhere to keep a dog," Neil chipped in.

"So they brought him to you," concluded Mike.

"They did," said Neil. "But what worries me is, who's going to want a pink dog? Who's going to give him a home looking like this? That's why we brought him to you. We thought you might know some way of getting the dye out."

Mike fingered the wiry pink hair. "I suppose you could try dyeing him again – a more sensible colour this time. But it's tricky stuff. You might end up with all his coat falling out. No, I think the best thing you can do is just wait for it to grow out."

"But he's only got two months," Emily said anxiously. "How long will it take?"

The local council, who helped to fund the rescue centre, were strict about the length of time dogs were allowed to stay there. If Bundle didn't find an owner before his two months were up, he would have to be put down.

Mike was about to reply when they heard Janice's raised voice from the reception area.

"I'm sorry, madam, but surgery is over for tonight. Let me book you an appointment for tomorrow."

Through the open surgery door, Neil saw a woman come into the waiting room, dragging a dog with her. Janice, looking flustered, appeared behind her.

"Thanks, Janice," Mike said, going through to them. "I'll see to it. Is there a problem with the dog, Mrs . . .?"

"Foster. Marjorie Foster."

The visitor was middle-aged, with curly brown hair, and she wore a smart business suit. Her face was red. She looked angry but at the same time also looked as if she was about to burst into tears.

"Yes, there is a problem with the dog," she said matter-of-factly. "I want you to put her to sleep."

Mike Turner stared at her for a moment.

Neil and Emily looked at each other, and then at her dog. She was a rough collie, with a long, intelligent face. Her beautiful, shaggy coat was amber and white, though she looked as if she hadn't been properly groomed for a long time. Mrs Foster was holding her on a tight lead, but the dog was straining to get away from her.

"I'm sorry, Mrs Foster," Mike said. "You can't just ask me to put a dog down if there's nothing the matter with it. I need a medical reason."

Mrs Foster tutted and looked even closer to tears. "But what am I going to do? I can't keep her, and I don't know anybody else who wants her." She jerked the lead. "Sit, Skye."

The dog's claws skittered on the floor. She didn't want to sit; she wanted to explore this interesting new place. Mike held out his hand to the collie, murmuring something soothing. Skye tried to jump up at him in a friendly way, but Mike gently pushed her down as he took the lead. Mrs Foster plumped down on a chair, took out a handkerchief and dabbed her eyes.

"Neil," Mike said, "look after Skye for a minute, will you? Janice, can you manage a cup of tea, please?" He sat down on the chair beside Mrs Foster. "Now, can you tell me what all this is about?"

Mrs Foster sat silently until Janice brought

the tea. Meanwhile Skye had caught sight of Bundle and Emily through the open surgery door and started forward to investigate. When Neil told her firmly to sit, she sat, looking round alertly.

"I'll keep Bundle in here," Emily shouted from the surgery.

"Skye is my father's dog," Marjorie Foster said at last, between sips of her tea. She was starting to look calmer. "He's had her for years – since she was a puppy. But now my father is an old man, and he can't cope with living on his own any more. A couple of days ago my husband and I moved him into a nursing home."

Neil watched Mrs Foster suddenly shoot a hostile glance at Skye.

"If it wasn't for that dog," she continued, "maybe he could have stayed in his own home a bit longer. She's a real handful, and Dad insisted on walking her in all weathers. In the end, she was just too much for him to cope with."

"And Skye couldn't go to the nursing home with your father?" asked Mike.

"No. They have a no pets policy."

"I'm afraid that's the case with a lot of

nursing homes. What does your father think about having Skye put down?"

Mrs Foster's face reddened. "He doesn't know," she admitted. "He thinks he'll be going back home one day, and that I'll look after Skye until then. But I knew I'd have to have her destroyed—"

"That's terrible!" Neil interrupted, unable to stop himself. "Taking an old man's dog away!"

Mrs Foster didn't reply.

"Is there a good reason why you can't keep Skye yourself?" asked Mike.

Marjorie Foster finished her tea and put the cup to one side. "We've looked after the dog before. I work at White and Marbeck, the solicitors in Compton, and my husband goes away a lot on business. It was difficult enough having her for a week, never mind permanently. The house is empty all day."

"Aah, I see," said the vet.

"Besides, my husband has an allergy to animal fur; his eyes start streaming if he goes anywhere near Skye. You see, it isn't as easy as it seems."

Once or twice, while Marjorie Foster was speaking, Skye had tried to wander off and explore the corners of the waiting room. Neil had needed all his authority to keep her sitting quietly. She was quite lively, and he could understand that she might be too much for an old man living alone. But there was no reason to think about killing her.

"You need the Puppy Patrol!" he said.

Mrs Foster gave him an unfriendly stare. "The Puppy Patrol? What on earth is that?"

"This is Neil Parker," Mike explained. "His parents, Bob and Carole, run King Street Kennels. You might have seen their green Range Rover in Compton. Some of their friends call them the Puppy Patrol."

"Oh . . . yes, maybe. But I'm afraid I can't afford to board Skye indefinitely. It's costing enough to keep Dad in the nursing home."

"We could take Skye to the rescue centre," Neil said eagerly. "We'd try to find her a new home. Somewhere she'd be really looked after."

Mrs Foster nodded slowly and her face brightened.

"That might be better . . . Skye would be fine with someone younger. And Dad might not mind losing her so much if he knew she was being properly looked after." A tear trickled down her face and she used her

11

handkerchief again. "I really don't want her to die, and Dad would never forgive me. Are you really sure . . .?"

"Oh yes," Neil said. "Skye's a lovely dog. We'll do anything we can to find her a new home."

Chapter Two

Next morning, a Saturday, the Parker family were eating breakfast round their big kitchen table. Sam, the family's black and white Border collie, lay under the table ready to hoover up any scattered cereal or bits of toast that might come his way.

Neil secretly slipped him a bit of sausage from his plate. Nobody looking at Sam now, with his glossy coat and alert expression, would think that he had been brought into the rescue centre as an abandoned puppy. That was four years ago, when Neil was only seven. Neil and his father had trained him, and Sam was now

13

almost unbeatable in Agility competitions at local country shows.

"Mike said he would ask his sister about Bundle's pink dye," Emily told her father. "She's a hairdresser and should be able to help. Mike thinks we'll have to let it grow out."

Bob Parker buttered himself a piece of toast. He was a big man with the same brown hair as Neil, though unlike Neil's, it was neatly combed. He wore an old pair of corduroy trousers and a green sweatshirt with the King Street Kennels logo emblazoned across the chest.

"It's not going to be that easy to find a home for Bundle," he said. "A couple came looking for a dog yesterday. As soon as they set eyes on Bundle, they burst out laughing and went away again."

"I think he looks lovely," said Sarah, Neil's five-year-old younger sister, with a toss of her black pigtails.

"You would," said Neil.

"And what about this other dog?" Bob asked. "This rough collie that you brought back last night? Your mother tells me you convinced the owner not to have her put down."

"Mrs Foster couldn't keep Skye. I had to offer her a place at the rescue centre. What else was I supposed to do?"

"You did the right thing, Neil," said Bob Parker. "But I don't think it's as simple as you might think. If Mrs Foster's father is Skye's legal owner, then where does that leave us if we find a new home for her? He might make a fuss. I'll have to give it some thought."

The telephone rang in the hallway.

"I'll get that," Carole Parker said, pushing her chair back.

A minute later, Neil heard her calling him. He swallowed the last mouthful of bacon and went through to the hallway. His mother was speaking on the phone and scribbling notes on the pad beside her. "Yes, as it happens we have one pen vacant – provided they'll be happy to be together . . ."

Neil could hear a distant voice talking at the other end of the line. His mother put her hand over the mouthpiece.

"Emergency, Neil. Last-minute booking," she whispered. "Could you get that vacant pen ready in Block Two?"

"Sure. Who is it?"

"No one I know. Two pekes." Carole spoke into the phone again. "Yes, Mrs Downes. You can bring them over right away. I shall need a current vaccination certificate and the week's fee in advance. And of course you're welcome to bring any baskets and toys, so that they'll feel more at home here. Yes . . . yes. We'll see you in half an hour or so, then."

Carole Parker put the phone down, stretched, and pushed her hair out of her eyes. "That's a good start to the weekend. Mrs

16

Downes' neighbour was supposed to be looking after her dogs while she went on holiday, but he fell off a ladder last night and is now in hospital."

"So the dogs are coming here. She's lucky we've got the space," Neil said.

"Yes, it is short notice. I'd rather she could come and visit first, but she has a plane to catch, so . . ." Carole shrugged. "I've got a stack of work to do, so it would be a real help if you could see to the pen, Neil. And keep a lookout for Mrs Downes and her pekes, will you?"

"Sure."

Neil went out and across the courtyard to the Kennel Blocks. Each block had two rows of ten pens on each side of a central aisle, and currently nearly every one was occupied.

He checked the empty pen and made sure that it was clean. Jumping up at the wire mesh on one side was Flossie, an excitable little Yorkshire terrier. She barked as Neil bent down and picked up the metal water bowl.

"Here, Floss, good girl," Neil said, giving her one of the dog treats which he always carried in his pocket.

On the other side of the empty pen was

Eddie, an elderly cocker spaniel, who lay with his nose on his paws and blinked peacefully at Neil through the mesh. Not even the thought of a dog treat could rouse him from his doze. He would be a quiet neighbour for the new arrivals, Neil thought.

Neil went out to the storeroom to fill the bowl with clean water. Kate McGuire, King Street's full-time kennel maid, was just starting to measure out the dogs' food for the early-morning feed. She was tall and slim, with a blonde ponytail, and Neil thought she looked nearly as bright as Bundle in her purple sweatshirt and striped leggings.

"Hi," he said. "I'll help you with that in a minute."

He told her about the two Pekinese they were expecting as he filled the bowl at the sink.

"I just hope they're not overfed, yappy little horrors," Kate said.

Neil grinned. He and Kate both liked dogs to be "proper" dogs – they had no patience with owners who made their pets look ridiculous with ribbons or fancy collars, or fed them unhealthy food like sweets and chocolate.

"I was reading about pekes the other night,"

Neil said. "They used to be called lion dogs. They were guard dogs for the Emperors of China, you know."

"No doubt they'll find this place a bit of a comedown, then," Kate said. "We'll have to be on our best behaviour."

When he'd finished preparing the pen for the new arrivals, Neil helped Kate feed the rest of the dogs in the boarding kennels. After that came the rescue centre. This was a smaller block, with fewer pens but the same basic facilities – each dog still had a spacious outside run to itself.

While they were working, he told Kate about Skye.

"I can't see why anybody would want to have a dog put down."

"But it's a real problem, isn't it?" Kate said, frowning. "If the old man can't look after her, and there's no one else . . ."

By now they were standing outside Skye's pen. The rough collie lay slumped in a corner. She looked unhappy. When Neil opened the door to take in the bowl of food, she raised her head, blinked and lay down again. Neil squatted down and stroked her nose.

"She's missing him," he said. "You don't know what it's all about, do you, Skye?"

"She's a lovely dog. There'll be plenty of people wanting her." Then Kate glanced over at bright pink Bundle, who was snuffling his way through his own food bowl in a pen opposite. "Not like some," she added.

"Skye could do with a good grooming," Neil said. "I'll look at her later."

"You'll have quite a job, then. Underneath that long hair there's another short thick coat. You'll have to get right down into that. Mind you, she should look terrific when you've finished."

Neil stroked her long orange and white coat admiringly. "Yes, she—"

He broke off as he heard Emily's voice shouting, "Neil! Neil!"

"In here!" he called.

Emily put her head round the door. "There's a phone call for you."

Neil raced to the office. Carole Parker was sitting at her desk with the phone in her outstretched hand.

"I think this is one you should deal with, Neil," she said, as if something was amusing her.

Neil took the phone. His mother went out with a pile of envelopes and left him to it.

"Hello. Neil Parker speaking."

"Hello." The speaker sounded like a young man. "You don't know me, but my name's Tom Dewhurst. I'm a helper at The Grange. I believe you've got Henry Bradshaw's dog."

Neil stood silent for a minute, his head spinning. "Henry Bradshaw's dog?" he queried.

"Yes," the man replied. "She's called Skye. I rang his daughter this morning, and she told me the dog was at King Street Kennels."

Neil began to understand. Henry Bradshaw must be Marjorie Foster's father. The Grange was an old people's home not far away, on the outskirts of Compton.

"That's right," Neil said. "Skye is here."

"Oh, thank goodness for that." Tom Dewhurst sounded relieved. "I wonder if you could do me a favour."

"Yes, if I can."

"Could you bring Skye round for a visit? Only Mr Bradshaw's getting very worried and upset about her. And, to be honest, he's been giving me a lot of grief. Ever since he got here, he's been wanting me to make sure she's all right. It's all he thinks about. Maybe if he could see her again he would settle down."

"Well . . ." Neil wasn't sure. He'd certainly like to bring Skye and Mr Bradshaw back together. But he knew it would distress Skye to be parted from the old man again, and the dog wouldn't be allowed to stay at The Grange.

"Please," Tom begged. "He's really getting very upset. It would certainly make my life a lot easier."

"Well . . . OK," Neil said, giving in. "When shall I come?"

"It's a bit difficult, you see . . ." Now it was Tom who sounded uneasy. "The Grange has a no pets policy. Matron's a real stickler about it. But just after lunch – say, between two and three – she works in her office, and . . ."

"Are you saying I have to smuggle Skye in to see him?"

"It's dead easy. Honest," Tom promised.

"She's a big dog, you know. I can't just stuff her up my jumper."

The more Neil heard about this idea, the less he liked it. If Matron was as strict as all that, somebody was going to get into trouble. He only hoped it wouldn't be him.

"If you come in through the main gates,"

22

Tom said, "and walk down the drive, you'll see a path going off to the left labelled 'Deliveries'. Go down there, and I'll meet you at the side door. There's nothing to it."

"All right," Neil said. "I'll be there. I just hope we're not going to be sorry about this."

Tom laughed. "Don't worry! See you!" He rang off.

As Neil left the office, a car turned into the gravel driveway in front of the house. It stopped and a woman got out. She was young, with short blonde hair; Neil had never seen her before, but he had a fairly good idea who she must be. He stepped forward.

"Mrs Downes?" he said. "I'll just call Mum. She's—"

"No, don't bother. I haven't time," the woman replied briskly. She was already pulling open the rear door of the car. The driver, a dark-haired man, stayed in his seat and kept the engine running.

"It won't take long," Neil said. "You'll want to see—"

"We'll miss our plane. Here!" The woman shoved two pet carriers into Neil's hands. She was tall and slim, with bright scarlet fingernails and lipstick, and high-heeled shoes. She was the sort of woman, Neil suspected, who would choose a dog to match her curtains.

"But you can't—"

Mrs Downes was still not listening. She took an envelope out of her handbag.

"Certificates. Cheque," she said, pushing them into Neil's hand along with the carriers. "We'll pick them up this time next week, OK?"

"But there's a card to fill in, and—"

Neil found he was speaking to thin air. The car door slammed. The engine roared. The wheels skidded round on the gravel, then the car took off in a cloud of dust and disappeared out of the gate. Neil was left standing in the drive clutching the two pet carriers.

"Hey," he said feebly.

He put the carriers down. In one of them he could see the flat black nose of a Pekinese dog pushed up against the grille. In the other he couldn't see anything, but he could hear a sound.

It wasn't a bark. It was a noise Neil had never heard a dog make – a kind of high-pitched howling. He bent down and peered through the grille.

Carole Parker came out onto the front

doorstep, followed by Emily and Sam. "What's going on?" she said. "What have you got there?"

Neil glanced up at her. "Mum," he said, "I really think you'd better come and look at this. It's a Siamese cat!"

Chapter Three

"A Siamese cat?" said Carole Parker in amazement. "We can't have a Siamese cat here!" She snatched the envelope from Neil, ripped it open and studied the contents.

"At least those are in order," she muttered. "But Neil, whatever were you thinking of? Why did you let her leave it here? Why didn't you call me?"

"You idiot, Neil," said Emily, laughing.

"It's not my fault," Neil said indignantly. "She just shoved the carriers into my hands and went. Anyway, you took the booking."

"For dogs!" replied his mother. "She told me—" Suddenly Carole Parker slapped her

26

forehead. "No – she said 'pets'. Had we room for her two little pets? And she mentioned Pekinese. I just assumed they were both . . . Do you know, I don't think that the wretched woman told me any lies at all. She let me believe they were dogs because she was desperate to get away on holiday. And now we're stuck with it."

Sam was sniffing curiously at the Pekinese behind the grille of the pet carrier, and Emily bent down to look at the cat, which was now sitting with brown paws tucked neatly under its creamy chest, blue eyes shining brilliantly in its chocolate-and-cream-coloured face. "It's not the cat's fault," she cooed. "I think it's sweet."

"You're starting to sound like Squirt," said Neil, raising his eyebrows.

"So what are we going to do with this cat?" Neil's mother stood looking down at the pet carrier with her hands on her hips. The cat stared back and let out another weird howling noise. "It doesn't even miaow like a proper cat!"

"Well, it can't share the pen with the peke," said Bob, looking over his wife's shoulder. "I suppose we could put it in the rescue centre. There's space there."

"And all the dogs will go berserk," Carole said. "Do you want to put up with that for a whole week?"

"Mum . . ." said Emily.

"Yes?"

"Could we have it in the house? Please?" Speaking faster, as if she could see that her mother was going to refuse, she went on, "I'd look after it and feed it. We could put a litter tray in the kitchen, and I'd clean it out. It wouldn't be any trouble."

"And what about Sam?" Neil objected. "The house is his place."

"Sam won't mind," Emily said. She stroked his glossy coat. "Will you, boy?"

Neil thought the cat had a smug look, almost as if it had been following the argument.

"The only thing that worries me," Carole said, "is what happens if it escapes? But then, why should I worry? I didn't ask for it in the first place. All right, Emily, we'll give it a try, for a day or two. But if it causes any trouble, we'll have to think again. I know a cattery over in Colshaw – it might have to go there."

Emily smiled and picked up the cat carrier. "What's its name?"

Carole looked at the vaccination certificates. "The peke is Ming. And that creature is a female called Tai-Lu. Keep her out from under my feet, that's all. I'm going to fill in the record cards." She gritted her teeth. "And I just can't wait for next Saturday, when Mrs Downes comes to pick up her two little pets."

She stalked off into the house. Emily followed her with Tai-Lu's carrier. Neil picked up Ming's.

"You're a beauty and too good for *that woman*," Neil muttered as he carried Ming through the side gate into the courtyard.

Ming jumped into the pen and went to touch noses through the wire with Flossie next door. Neil put the carrier and the spare bowl away, and brought a basket and bedding from the storeroom When he got back to the kennel block he found his father looking in at Ming through the wire mesh.

"Nothing much wrong with him," Bob said, nodding. "How's that Skye of yours doing?"

Neil remembered that in all the confusion of the cat's arrival, he hadn't told his parents about the phone call from Tom Dewhurst.

"Only go if you're sure a visit might help," Bob said, when Neil had finished explaining his plans. "If Mr Bradshaw has to let go, it might be kinder to make a clean break."

"I thought that too at first, but Skye's *his* dog," Neil protested.

"Yes . . . but it's what Skye needs that we have to think of now."

"What Skye needs now is a good grooming," Neil said. "Is it OK if I do it?"

"I'll give you a hand."

Neil fetched Skye from the rescue centre. She brightened up once she was out of the pen, looking around eagerly. Without her lead she would have investigated every nook and cranny between the rescue centre and the storeroom.

By the time Neil arrived, Bob had got out the grooming equipment from the store. The treatment room was used for grooming as well; Carole liked to send the boarding dogs home looking as presentable as possible.

Bob put the ramp in place so Skye could stand on the table.

"She's been neglected," he told Neil. "Not seriously – she's healthy enough and well fed, but look at her feet. Her nails haven't been clipped for a long time. And her teeth – if my teeth looked like that, my dentist would have a fit."

Bob began to trim Skye's nails with clippers.

"You have to be very careful not to cut into the quick," he explained to Neil. "That's the fleshy part underneath the nail. If you don't watch out you could really hurt her."

"I've never had to trim Sam's nails," Neil said.

"That's because Sam gets a lot of exercise on roads, which wears his nails down. I bet Skye has been walked over fields."

Skye stood quietly while her nails were trimmed, but cleaning her teeth was another matter. She didn't like that at all. She backed away from Bob, and Neil had to keep a firm hold of her to stop her slipping off the end of the table.

"She's not the best behaved dog I've ever seen. But at least she's not trying to bite me. There. That'll do. She'll have clean breath now."

Skye showed off her gleaming teeth, almost as if she understood what he was saying.

"Right, Neil," Bob said. "You can do the next bit. Give her a good spray, and work it well into her coat."

The grooming spray was made up of disinfectant and water. Neil showered Skye with the spray and rubbed it in, then he began to brush her coat with the flat slicker brush, working against the lie of the coat, from the tail up to the head, until Skye looked like a vast dandelion clock. He remembered what Kate had said about the thick undercoat; it was matted, and the long hair was full of snarls and tangles as if no one had brushed her thoroughly for a long time.

"Now the fun bit," said Bob.

Neil began combing the hair in the right direction this time, working from the tail again so that the coat fell in long, silky folds, all the tangles teased out.

"She loves it," Bob said. "You know you're a real smasher, don't you, Skye? Right, Neil, just trim the hair round her feet and hocks – the joints there on the hind legs – and you're done."

Neil's back was aching and he was sweating from the hard work, but when he stood back and looked at Skye it was worth it.

*

When Neil walked into the kitchen at
lunchtime with Sam at his heels, he found
Tai-Lu curled up asleep in the old basket
chair by the window, Sam's favourite place.

Sam trotted over and looked at her, and
then cocked his head at Neil as if he was
asking what that strange creature was doing
in his chair.

"I know," Neil said. "It's not fair, is it?"

Sam poked his head forward, sniffing
cautiously. Sapphire eyes opened. A chocolate
paw shot out. Sam sprang backwards with a

whimpering noise, nearly tripping Bob, who was bringing a pan of spaghetti sauce from the cooker to the table.

"Look what your cat's done!" Neil said to Emily, who was sitting at the table. "If she's scratched Sam . . ."

Sam had slunk under the table. Neil had to get down on his hands and knees to look, but to his relief he couldn't see any marks on Sam's nose.

"He's OK," he said, getting to his feet again and glowering at Emily. "Just watch that cat, that's all."

"She's frightened because she's in a strange place," said Emily.

"Frightened? Huh!"

He took his seat at the table as Bob finished serving out the spaghetti sauce.

"OK, Neil," said Carole. "I'm sorry about the cat, but we'll all have to put up with it, even Sam. It's only for a week. Sarah, stop practising now and come and eat your lunch."

Sarah, who had been using the back of her chair as a barre to practise her ballet steps, slid into her seat beside Neil.

"I think it's a horrid cat," she said. "It wants to eat my Fudge."

Neil was surprised to find his little sister on his side for once. He hadn't thought about Fudge, her hamster, but she was right. If Tai-Lu got her paws on him . . . no more Fudge.

"You'll have to make sure you close your bedroom door, love," Carole said. "Fudge will be fine if you're careful. And Neil – if you're going to slurp spaghetti like that, I'll give you a bowl on the floor."

"Sorry," Neil said, slowing very slightly the rate he was shovelling in spaghetti. "I've got to take Skye to see her owner. Sam can come too – out of the way of that cat!"

When lunch was over, Neil fetched Skye and put her on the lead. Freshly groomed, with her silky coat and trimmed nails, she looked a very handsome dog.

"Mr Bradshaw's going to be really impressed when he sees you, Skye," Neil said. "It's a shame you can't stay."

He whistled for Sam, who shot out of his favourite hiding place under the hedge at the bottom of the garden. At least the cat couldn't chase him out of there, Neil thought.

He let Sam run free as they went through the gate into the exercise field. The easiest way to get to The Grange was by footpaths that followed the foot of the ridgeway to Compton, and it would make a good run for the dogs.

Sam darted off, though he never went far from Neil. Skye whined softly, as if she would have liked to run free, too, but Neil didn't know her well enough to be happy about letting her off the lead. At first she tried to dash after Sam, but once she realized that Neil wouldn't put up with any nonsense she walked obediently to heel.

The walk to The Grange took about half an hour. The last footpath led over a stile into a road alongside a high stone wall.

"Sam!" Neil called.

Sam came at once, and sat at Neil's feet while he clipped on his lead. Then they followed the wall until they came to a pair of wrought-iron gates, standing open. Fixed to the wall was a sign that read:

The Grange
RESIDENTIAL HOME FOR THE ELDERLY

Neil led the dogs up to the gates. Ahead of him was a curving drive, bordered by shrubs.

Lawns stretched off to the left and right, but the house itself was hidden behind trees. No one was in sight. The only sounds were birdsong and the wind in the branches.

For the first time Neil wondered if it had been a good idea to bring Sam. But then he would be in trouble for smuggling in just one dog if the Matron caught him, so he might as well be in trouble for two. Besides, he wasn't going to leave Sam to be tormented by that wretched cat!

Looking round cautiously, Neil led the dogs through the gates.

"OK," he said. "Here we go."

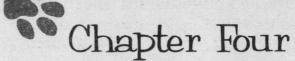

Chapter Four

N eil felt uneasy as he walked up the drive. Both dogs trotted calmly at heel, as if they knew they had to be on their best behaviour.

Before long, a turn in the drive brought Neil within sight of the house. He stood still for a minute and looked.

The Grange old people's home was a long grey building, with three floors and steps leading up to an imposing front door. The windows sparkled in the sunlight, and bright flower beds stretched all along the front of the house.

Neil was impressed. He hadn't expected The Grange to be quite so grand. Surely with all that space they could find room for one not-especially-big dog?

A little further on the drive divided. The path to the left was signposted "Deliveries" as Tom Dewhurst had said. Neil followed it.

The path wound through shrubbery, leading round the side of the house. Neil arrived at a gravelled space and what looked like a kitchen door with bins outside. A small van was parked there.

Neil hesitated, uncertain of where to go next. There was still no one around. This must be the place where Tom had promised to meet him, so where was he?

Skye was starting to get restless again, tugging at the lead, clearly wanting to investigate some enticing smell from the kitchen or the bins.

"Sit, Skye," Neil said firmly. Skye looked up at him, jaws parted. "Yes, you," Neil insisted. "Sit."

Skye sat. At the same moment the kitchen door opened, and a young man appeared. He was thin and wiry, and wore jeans and a T-shirt; he didn't look any older than Kate McGuire.

"Hi," he said, grinning widely. "You must be

Neil. I'm Tom Dewhurst. And this is Skye?" He squatted down and plunged his hands into Skye's ruff. "Wow, you're a beautiful—"

Skye objected. She pulled back, and Tom, caught off balance, sat down hard in the dust.

"Hey, doesn't she like me?" he said.

"She wants you to be more polite," Neil said, trying to keep a straight face.

"Oh. Right." Tom got up, brushed himself off and swept Skye an elaborate bow. "I beg your pardon, ma'am."

"Never startle a dog you don't know," Neil said, feeling Tom was in need of advice. "That's the way to get bitten."

"But I feel I do know Skye," Tom said. "I've heard such a lot about her from Mr Bradshaw. And who's this?" he added, indicating Sam.

Neil introduced the Border collie. To his relief, Tom didn't seem worried about him bringing in another dog. Learning from his bad start with Skye, he bent down and patted Sam cautiously. Sam wagged his tail.

"Good boy," Tom said, and laughed as Neil gave Sam a dog treat and Skye came nosing in for a share.

Straightening up, he quickly glanced

around and then beckoned to Neil. "Come on. This way."

He led Neil and the dogs down another path, narrower this time, with thick shrubs arching overhead. Soon they turned the corner of the house and came out into the open.

A smooth green lawn stretched down to trees about a hundred metres away. At the sides were stone walls covered with climbing plants. At the back of the house, steps led up to a stone terrace, with groups of cushioned chairs. A few people were sitting there, with one or two walking on the lawn.

"Wow!" Neil said. "This is great."

"Not bad, is it?"

Neil was thinking what a wonderful place this would be for a dog to run about in. It seemed such a waste that no pets were allowed. He was going to ask Tom who had made such a stupid rule, when Skye gave a sudden, sharp bark. She jerked at her lead. Neil was not expecting it and she pulled the loop out of his hand.

"Skye!" he shouted.

Skye was running towards the terrace, straight as an arrow. One of the old men

sitting there had got up from his seat. Skye
leapt up the steps and hurled herself at him.
The man's arms went round her.

"That's Mr Bradshaw," said Tom.

Neil didn't need telling. Skye had known
right away who he was, and where she wanted
to be.

He followed Tom up to the terrace. By the
time they got there, Mr Bradshaw was sitting
down again, with Skye's muzzle resting on his
knee. He was stroking her head.

"Eh, Tom, lad," he said, as the boys came
up. "Didn't I tell you she were a grand
dog?"

"You did, Mr Bradshaw," Tom agreed. "And she is. This is Neil – he's looking after Skye at the moment."

Mr Bradshaw leant over to shake hands with Neil. He had thick white hair and a bristling moustache. Neil noticed that his clothes hung loosely on him and the veins on his hands stood out like cords.

"Helping out our Marjorie, are you?" the old man said.

"Yes, sir, that's right."

Neil didn't know how to explain his situation properly. Mr Bradshaw and Skye looked so happy together, Neil couldn't bear to spoil it.

The other residents in the garden were gathering round to admire Skye. One or two of them gave her sweets and biscuits, which really wasn't very good for her. Sam came in for his share of the attention too; Neil had to tell himself that it wouldn't hurt, just this once.

Mr Bradshaw started telling stories about how clever Skye was; all Tom and Neil could do was sit on the steps and listen. Sam had settled happily at the feet of an old lady who kept patting him and talking to him.

"He can stand any amount of that," Neil said.

"Yes, he—"

Suddenly Neil noticed that Tom's expression had changed. His eyes widened and he scrambled to his feet. "That's torn it," he muttered.

Neil turned. At the back of the terrace, French windows led into a sitting room. A woman was standing there, looking out. Neil thought she looked about two metres tall.

"Matron," Tom said in a hollow voice.

Neil got to his feet as well.

"I thought you said she would be working in her office?"

"She is. She should be."

The woman opened the French window and stepped out. She was wearing a dark blue dress which reminded Neil of a nurse's uniform, and had grey hair coiled neatly on the top of her head. Tom walked over to her and Neil followed.

"Good afternoon," she said. Her voice was pleasant, though her face remained disapproving. "Who is this, Tom?"

Tom gave a twitchy grin.

"Visitors, Matron."

"I can see that. You do know, don't you, Tom, that all visitors are supposed to report to reception?"

Tom looked at his feet.

"Yes, Matron."

"There are very good reasons for that rule. Some of our residents are easily upset, and I need to know who is on the premises."

"Yes, Matron."

"So introduce your visitors to me, Tom."

Rather hesitantly, Tom introduced Neil, and told Matron about Skye and Sam. Matron unbent slightly.

"Parker . . . from King Street Kennels?"

"Yes, that's right," Neil replied. "My mum and dad run it."

"My niece's dog stayed with you last year, I believe. She said how well looked after he was."

Neil felt better after he heard that, and Tom started to relax. For a moment, Matron watched the group of old people around the dogs.

"A beautiful animal," she said admiringly. "I thought Mr Bradshaw's daughter was looking after her. Is she boarding Skye with you?"

"No," Neil said. "Skye's in the rescue

centre." As Matron clearly didn't know what that meant, he explained. "It's where dogs without owners go. We find new homes for them."

"But . . ." Matron looked across at Mr Bradshaw, who was still sitting with his hand possessively on Skye's head.

"You won't tell him, will you?" Neil said. "Not yet, anyway."

Matron shook her head. She looked sympathetic. "I won't say a word," she promised. "But he'll have to know, sooner or later."

Neil sensed that Sam was starting to get restless. Skye, however, was sitting contentedly up against Mr Bradshaw's knee, and when Neil came to take her lead she was reluctant to move.

"Nay, lass," said Mr Bradshaw, affectionately. "It's time to go." He gave Neil a direct look with his bright blue eyes. "You'll bring her again, won't you, lad?"

"Yes, I will," he said. "I promise."

"But let us know you're coming next time," Matron added, smiling.

When Mr Bradshaw told her to go, Skye allowed Neil to lead her away, though she kept looking back. Tom took Neil round to the front of the house.

"I'd have Skye like a shot," he said miserably. "And I'd bring her to see Mr Bradshaw. But it's no good. I live in a third-floor flat. It wouldn't be fair on her."

"I guess not," Neil said.

Tom bent down and gave Skye and Sam another pat before Neil led the dogs out through the gates. He was still watching as they walked down the road.

Once over the stile and on to the footpath, Neil let Sam off the lead again. He bounded off into the grass. Skye gave Neil an imploring look.

At first Neil ignored her, but as they walked on and Skye kept to heel without any fuss, he began to have second thoughts. After all, she had behaved beautifully at The Grange.

"All right, Skye," he said, bending down to unclip the lead. "Go and play with Sam."

Skye gave a bark of pleasure as she was freed. She shot off after Sam, and Neil watched the two dogs leaping around, chasing each other and rolling on the ground. Neil grinned. This was how he liked to see dogs.

When he had watched them playing for a

few minutes he whistled and called to Sam. The black and white Border collie came running back to his side.

"Skye!" Neil called.

Instead of obeying, Skye kept on running through the long grass. Neil struggled to keep her in sight.

"Skye! Come back!"

Skye took no notice. Neil started to run after her.

"Sam!" he yelled. "Fetch!"

Sam took off at once, powerful muscles bunching and stretching, easily outstripping Neil. Charging along behind, Neil saw Skye appear from the grass at the edge of the field, wriggle under the fence and hurl herself, an orange streak, diagonally up the hill that led to the ridgeway. Seconds later, Sam followed. By the time Neil reached the fence, both dogs had disappeared among the bushes at the top of the hill.

Neil climbed after them. His breath was coming in painful gasps by the time he reached the top. Sam erupted from the bushes as Neil drew close, but there was no sign of Skye.

"Where is she, Sam?" Neil panted. "Find!"

Sam tried his best. He ran back and forth in short bursts, nose to the ground, whimpering occasionally, but he didn't know which way to go. Neil patted him.

"Never mind," he said. "You're not a tracker dog, Sam. It's not your fault."

Neil searched among the trees and bushes, calling Skye's name as he went. There was no response. He came to a halt at last, looking towards Compton from the top of the hill. He could see the town in the distance, and just below him was the exercise field he knew so well, and King Street Kennels itself. But nothing moved in the landscape ahead. Skye had gone.

Chapter Five

Neil plodded down the hill towards the kennels. As he went he kept on looking for Skye and calling her name, but without much hope. By now she could be anywhere.

He let himself in through the field gate and crossed the courtyard to the house. In the kitchen, his mother was sitting at the table drinking tea, looking at a picture that Sarah was painting. Neil thought it looked like a strawberry ice cream.

"Look, Neil," Sarah said proudly. "I'm painting Bundle."

"That's great, Squirt."

His mother gave him a sharp look.

"What's the matter with you?"

There was no way of hiding it. Neil took a deep breath. "I've lost Skye," he confessed.

"What? How?"

Carole was interrupted by Emily, who bounced into the room saying, "I've spoken to him, and he says—"

She broke off in her turn as she realized something was wrong.

"I've lost Skye," Neil repeated.

Emily stared at him.

"What happened?" Carole asked.

Neil told the story of how he had let Skye off the lead on the way back from The Grange, and how she had disappeared in the bushes at the top of the hill.

"Do you want to go and look?" Emily said. "I'll come with you and help."

"Just a minute," Carole said. "Let's think before you start dashing off. Where is Skye likely to go?"

"Back to Mr Bradshaw," Neil said. "She didn't want to leave him. Those two really love each other."

Even as he spoke, he wasn't sure. Skye hadn't run back towards The Grange, not while she was still in sight.

51

"They'll ring if she turns up there," Carole said. "She wouldn't go back to the daughter's house, would she?"

"No way!" Emily was indignant.

"She was only there a couple of days," Neil said. "She wouldn't remember it."

"Poor Skye," said Sarah, splodging more pink paint on her picture of Bundle.

"But she would remember her own home," Emily said. "Where she lived with Mr Bradshaw. Maybe she went there."

Neil felt a sudden stab of hope. That made sense. Skye had probably recognized where Mr Bradshaw used to walk her and would know her way home. The only problem was that Neil had no idea where Mr Bradshaw had lived before he moved to The Grange.

"Tom might have his address," he suggested.

"No, try the phone book," Carole said. "Mr Bradshaw only moved a few days ago. He'll still be listed."

Emily had already gone to fetch the book from the hallway. She flipped it open and started turning pages.

"There are loads of Bradshaws," she said grimly.

"His name's Henry," Neil told her. "Look under H."

Emily ran her finger down the column.

"HD . . . no, that's a vicar. HM . . . 5 Derwent Mansions . . ."

"That's a block of flats," Carole said.

"Mrs Foster talked about a cottage," Neil said.

"Here it is!" Emily said triumphantly. "Bradshaw, HS, 11 Rookery Lane. That must be him – and it's not far from here."

"And there's a footpath from there leading up onto the ridgeway!" Neil added.

"Can we go, Mum?" Emily asked.

Carole thought for a minute.

"OK, take your bikes," she said. "Kate's gone home, and your dad's not here, or I'd give you a lift. I'll stay by the phone, in case there's any news. But if you don't find her," she continued, "we'll have to get in touch with the police."

Neil felt better as he and Emily set off on their bikes. At least he was doing something. It helped him fight his guilt and anger about how stupid he had been to let Skye off the lead.

"Just before you came home, I rang the

Compton News," Emily said when they were on their way. "I spoke to Jake Fielding. He's going to come and do a story about Bundle."

"That's good," Neil said, lost in thought.

A pink dog was certainly news, Neil figured. Jake had often helped with publicity for the rescue centre, and they had found homes for several dogs through stories in the local paper. Perhaps they would find a home for Bundle as well.

"And how's the cat?" he asked.

"Fine, so far. She slept all afternoon." Emily gave her brother a sideways grin. "Mum still calls her 'that creature', though."

Rookery Lane was a narrow road leading uphill. On one side were old cottages, built of the local grey stone, with tiny front gardens. On the other side was a drystone wall, with a field beyond it swelling gently to the horizon. Sheep cropped the short moorland grass.

The surface of the lane was uneven, so Neil and Emily got off their bikes and pushed them up the hill.

Rookery Lane came to an end just beyond the row of cottages. The road stopped at a cattle grid and a five-bar gate.

Number 11 was the last cottage. Curtains still hung at the windows but there was an empty feeling about it. The paintwork was cracked and blistered. The little garden was overgrown with weeds; Neil supposed that Mr Bradshaw had not been able to look after it properly for some time. Beside the gate was an estate agent's "For Sale" board, with a "Sold" sign tacked over it.

"The new people aren't here yet," Emily said.

"Nor is Skye," Neil replied, looking around.

The path led up to a porch. Neil and Emily leant their bikes against the fence, pushed their way through the creaky gate and walked up to the door. Emily knocked, but neither of them expected a reply. Neil peered through the right-hand window.

It was a sitting room. Two old leather chairs stood on either side of an empty fireplace. There was a rag rug in front of the fire. Beside it Neil could see a dog basket, with a piece of blanket lining it and a rubber bone abandoned inside.

He could imagine the fire lit, and Mr Bradshaw reading the newspaper, while Skye dozed contentedly in her basket.

He joined Emily at the other window, which looked into a kitchen with an old-fashioned cooker and sink, and a table with a high-backed chair.

"Skye couldn't have got inside," Emily said in despair.

"Let's look round the back."

Neil had to go on hoping up to the last minute. On the way he had convinced himself that Skye must be here, and he didn't know what he would do if she wasn't. He couldn't face the thought of going home without her.

He forced his way through the weeds as far as a patch of rough ground behind the cottage. There was a tumbledown shed and a gnarled old apple tree in one corner.

"Skye!" he called. "Skye!"

There was no answering bark. Instead Neil heard another sound – the sharp crack of a shotgun. He was not sure where it came from.

He hurried back to Emily in the front garden. She pointed across the lane, to where the sheep on the hillside were bleating and scattering.

"Neil! It came from over there!" she cried.

Another shot cracked out. Over the brow of

the hill a dog appeared, racing along at full stretch, low to the ground.

"Skye!" Neil yelled.

He hurled himself at the five-bar gate and climbed over, diving to intercept Skye as she came dashing towards him. Emily scrambled after him. Skye swerved; it was Emily who grabbed her collar and held her while Neil clipped on the lead.

When Skye was safe, Neil became aware of loud shouting. A man was running down the hill towards them, waving a shotgun.

"No! Get back!" he bellowed.

Skye bounded forward, pulling to the length of the lead. Her eyes stared, wild with terror.

"Sit, Skye," said Neil sharply.

Skye did not sit, but she stopped tugging, and stood trembling beside Neil.

The man slid down the last few metres and came to a halt in front of them. He was tall and broad-shouldered, about the same age as their father, with a freckled face and thick brown hair. Neil thought he must be the farmer who owned the land.

"What do you kids think you're doing?" His voice was loud and angry. "You could have got yourselves shot."

"I'm sorry, we—"

The farmer was not listening. "Come away from that dog," he ordered. "It's dangerous."

Skye was panting rapidly, her tongue lolling out. She was starting to calm down though she was still nervous.

"She's not dangerous," Neil said. "You've frightened the life out of her, that's all."

"Is she your dog?"

"No, but—"

"Then stand away from her."

The farmer cocked his shotgun and sighted down the barrels.

"No!" Emily screamed.

Neil pushed Skye's lead into her hand. All at once he was frightened, angry and confused, and he hardly knew what he was doing. He stepped between Skye and the gun.

"You stupid . . ."

The farmer lowered the gun so that the barrels pointed to the ground. He slipped on the safety catch. He looked like a man barely able to hold on to his temper.

"What do you think you're playing at?"

"You're not going to shoot Skye," Neil said determinedly.

"Skye?" The farmer stared at her. "That's

old Mr Bradshaw's dog. I thought I recognized her. What's she doing here?"

"We—" Neil started to explain again, but the farmer still wasn't listening.

"Now look," he said. "That dog's dangerous. She's on my land, worrying my sheep, and I've got every right to shoot her. So get out of the way. I don't want anybody getting hurt."

"We don't want Skye getting hurt," Emily said. "She hasn't done any harm."

"Hasn't done any harm?" the farmer repeated. "You don't know what you're talking

about, young miss. That dog has just killed one of my sheep."

Emily gasped. Neil stared at the farmer.

"She wouldn't," he said, alarmed. "I don't believe it."

The farmer snorted. "Have you had a good look at her?" he asked.

Neil turned round and had a proper look at Skye for the first time since she came flying over the hill. She was no longer the beautifully groomed dog she had been earlier in the day. Her coat was tangled and, worst of all, there were flecks of blood round her muzzle and spattered over her ruff.

"Oh, Skye . . ." Emily's words were almost a sob.

The farmer jerked his head. "Come and see."

Neil and Emily looked at each other, and then followed him up the hill, dragging a reluctant Skye. When they came to the top, the farmer stopped and pointed. "There."

A few metres away, further down the slope, a sheep was lying on its side. Neil could see the brutal red of torn flesh, and blood soaking the greyish-white fleece. Flies buzzed over the open wound.

Beside the sheep a dog was standing on guard – an Airedale terrier. The farmer whistled, and immediately it ran up to him and sat at his feet. The farmer patted it.

"Good boy, Shandy." His voice was quieter now. He went on, "I don't want to destroy the dog. But this is the third time this has happened in the last fortnight. It can't go on."

"Did you actually see Skye kill the sheep, sir?" Neil asked.

The farmer shook his head. "No. I found it dead, with that dog nosing around inside it. What am I supposed to think?"

"There must be a mistake," Neil said. "Skye's not dangerous."

"How would you like it if somebody shot your dog?" Emily demanded.

The farmer patted his Airedale again. "I love dogs," he said. "I've sacked a man before now for ill-treating a dog of mine. But sometimes you get a bad apple in the barrel and then there's nothing else for it." He slapped the stock of the gun. "I'm sorry."

"You're not going to shoot Skye," Emily said. "We won't let you."

"What if we take her home," Neil suggested, "and make sure she can't get out again? My

61

dad runs King Street Kennels – we can keep her in a pen. She won't give you any more trouble, I promise."

The farmer's eyes were hard. "A dangerous dog is a dangerous dog," he said. "What if she attacked you?"

"She won't. I know she won't." Neil knew it was time to act positively to save Skye's life. "I'm sorry, but I'm taking Skye home. You can't shoot her without hurting us. I'll tell my father what's happened and get him to phone you."

The farmer let out his breath and shook his head. Neil didn't wait to hear his reply. He turned away, letting Skye walk in front of him. Emily fell in beside him, helping to shield her.

As he opened the gate to let them through, Neil looked back. The farmer and his dog were still watching from the top of the hill.

"You'll hear more about this!" he shouted.

Neil ignored him, and led Skye through the gate into Rookery Lane.

Neil and Emily collected their bikes and walked home in silence with Skye loping alongside. As Neil turned into the drive, his heart lurched.

Parked in front of the house was a police dog van.

Chapter Six

Neil and Emily stared at the dog van.

"It can't be . . ." Emily said.

"There's been time, if the farmer phoned them as soon as we left. I told him we came from King Street Kennels." Neil swallowed and squared his shoulders. "We'd better go in."

As soon as he opened the door and went into the hall, Neil heard his father's voice, calling from the office.

"Neil, is that you? In here."

Bob Parker was sitting behind the desk, and opposite him was Sergeant Moorhead from the local police. Neil had met him before, but did not know him very well. He was a middle-aged man with grey hair clipped very short. He had put his peaked cap on the desk in front of him, and he had his notebook out.

"Neil. Emily." He nodded curtly. "And this is the dog?"

Emily was standing in the doorway, with Skye on the lead. Gently she drew the dog into the room to stand in front of the sergeant.

Sergeant Moorhead looked her over and reached out to tease one of the spots of blood out of her coat. Skye jerked her head away and let out a soft growling from deep in her throat. The sergeant drew his hand back rapidly.

"She's upset, sir," Neil said.

The sergeant grunted. He rubbed the dried blood between his fingertips, sniffed it, and made a note in his book.

"Right," he said crisply. "Let's hear your side of it."

Neil glanced at his father. He wasn't sure how much he already knew.

"Start from when you left The Grange with Skye," Bob said.

Neil began. Sergeant Moorhead kept interrupting to ask questions, so the whole story took a long time. Skye flopped down on the floor, looking as placid as Neil could have hoped for. Soon Carole came in with a cup of coffee which she placed on the desk beside the sergeant, then she sat down on the other side of the room.

"The farmer was Geoffrey Milton," Sergeant Moorhead said at last, when Neil had finished. "You were up on Causeway Farm. His land runs all along Rookery Lane. He was furious that you interfered when he wanted to shoot the dog, and then took her away without his permission."

"I wasn't going to let him shoot Skye," Neil said. "She's not dangerous."

"Mr Milton says differently." The sergeant drank some of his coffee. "For what it's worth, Neil, you had every right to do that. The law would let Mr Milton shoot a dog worrying sheep on his own land, provided that was the only reasonable way of stopping it. Once someone turns up to control the dog, he's not allowed to kill it."

Neil felt his knees go weak with relief.

"Then it's all right?" he said.

Sergeant Moorhead leant forward. "No, young man. It's very far from all right. Geoffrey Milton found Skye nosing over a dead sheep on his land. What's more, he lost two more sheep the same way, a week ago. What can you tell me about that?"

"Nothing," Neil said. "Skye would still have been with Mr Bradshaw then."

The sergeant obviously didn't know what Neil was talking about, and Bob Parker brought him up to date with the story of how Skye came to be at King Street Kennels.

"So what it boils down to," Sergeant Moorhead said, scribbling rapidly, "is that the dog was living in Rookery Lane in the care of an old man who everybody agrees was incapable of controlling it."

"It wasn't like that!" Neil protested.

"Then you tell me what it was like."

Neil looked helplessly at his father.

"Dad, I'm sorry. What are we going to do? What's going to happen to Skye?"

"I know she didn't kill those sheep!" Emily said, nearly in tears.

"Just calm down," Bob said. "Sergeant, remind us how we stand legally."

"Right." Sergeant Moorhead rested his hands on his knees. "If a dog trespasses on someone else's land, and kills or injures livestock – as this dog has done—"

"As Mr Milton says this dog has done," Neil interrupted swiftly.

The sergeant acknowledged the interruption with a nod.

"If a dog does that, then the keeper of the dog is responsible. He can be prosecuted and fined, and he's liable for the cost of the damage."

"What about the dog?" Emily asked. She was sitting on the floor beside Skye and had thrown an arm round her neck, as if she was protecting her.

"I'll come to that in a minute," Sergeant Moorhead said. "Now, the keeper of the dog is usually the owner, but in a case like this, where the owner passed on the dog to another responsible person, then—"

"But that was me!" Neil interrupted again. "I was looking after Skye." It was an effort to keep his voice steady. "Does that mean I'll have to go to court?"

"No. Because you're under sixteen, as far as the law's concerned the responsible person is the head of the household. Your father."

"But that's not fair!" Neil said. "I let Skye go. It was my fault."

Neil felt sick. He hardly listened as his

father and Sergeant Moorhead discussed the legal implications. If only he hadn't let Skye off the lead – all this would never have happened.

Neil started to pay attention again as he realized that his father was talking about Skye.

"Look at her," he was saying. "You're not telling me the dog's vicious!"

Sergeant Moorhead looked down at the sleepy, contented Skye, her muzzle resting on her paws and her eyes half closed.

"Well, she doesn't look vicious now," he said. "But I'll tell you, Mr Parker, I wouldn't want children of mine near her."

"What's going to happen to her?" Neil asked.

"It's best if she comes with me."

"No!" Emily leapt to her feet. Her voice rose in outrage.

"Can you do that?" Neil said. "She'll be safe in one of our pens. She won't get away."

"She got away once, didn't she?" the sergeant said drily. Neil flushed and was silent.

"Sergeant, you're not going to hurt the dog, are you?" Carole asked.

"No, she'll be quite safe. She'll be kept

under control until the court case comes up. You'll be informed about when that is."

"And then what?" Bob asked.

"That's up to the magistrate. He might make an order for the dog to be kept under proper control. Or alternatively . . ." The sergeant passed a hand over his thinning hair. For the first time he looked as if this was more than just a legal problem that it was his job to settle. "I'm sorry, but the magistrate might decide that the dog should be destroyed."

Neil and his father followed Sergeant Moorhead out of the office. Emily had burst into tears and Carole had stayed to comfort her.

Sergeant Moorhead led Skye to the police van and she was no trouble to him; Neil thought she must be feeling too tired to be difficult. She whimpered when he opened the door of the police van, and jumped into the back with only a very brief hesitation. Sergeant Moorhead slammed the door.

"I'll be in touch."

"You'll look after her, won't you?" Neil said. For the first time the sergeant smiled. "Of course we will. She'll be fine."

Neil could see Skye gazing out of the back window as the van left. Her long, intelligent face looked puzzled. To Neil it felt as if she was going to prison.

He and his father watched until the police van was out of sight.

"Dad, why did you let him take her?" Neil said.

"It's always best to co-operate with the police," Bob Parker said. "We're in enough trouble without starting an argument."

Neil scuffed his feet in the dust of the drive.

"Dad, I'm really sorry."

"Now let's get this straight." Bob stuck his hands in his pockets and faced his son. "You

70

haven't done anything wrong, Neil. OK, you made a mistake when you let Skye off the lead, but we all make mistakes. Nothing that anybody said to us suggested that Skye might be dangerous." He ran a hand through his hair. "In fact, I'd have sworn she wasn't dangerous. Lively, but not vicious."

"Do you think she killed those sheep, Dad?"

Bob Parker shook his head. "I don't know, Neil. I just don't know."

Slowly they started to walk back to the house.

"If they put her to sleep," Neil said, "I don't know what we'll tell Mr Bradshaw. He really loves her."

"Yes. And the worst of it is, if she's not destroyed it's going to be that much harder to find her a new owner. I'd have to tell the truth about her."

"So she'd be put down anyway when her time at the rescue centre is up?"

Bob had no reply to that, but there was no need for one. Neil could not see any hope for Skye.

"And that's not the only thing . . ." Bob sounded as if he was thinking aloud, but then he broke off with a sideways look at Neil.

"Dad?"

His father shook his head.

"I don't want to worry you."

"I'll worry a lot more if you don't tell me."

They came to the bottom of the steps, where Bob stopped. "Well . . . but you don't say anything to Emily, OK? The thing is, Neil, if I'm convicted of not keeping a dangerous dog under proper control, what's going to happen when the licence for the kennels comes up for renewal? What are the magistrates going to think about me then?"

Neil felt a tightness across his chest. In his worst nightmares he had never thought of this.

"Dad – do you mean that King Street Kennels might have to close down?"

Chapter Seven

"Close us down? It's possible. But I don't think it'll come to that." Bob Parker clapped Neil on the shoulder. "Come on. Try to put a smile on your face for Emily."

Neil followed his father up the steps to the door. As they went in, they heard a scream from Sarah's bedroom, and she came crashing down the stairs.

"Mummy! Mummy!" she was yelling.

Bob caught her at the foot of the stairs as Carole appeared in the doorway of the sitting room.

"Sarah, what's the matter?" she said.

"Mummy, it's Fudge!" Sarah was sobbing so

hard she could hardly get the words out. "The cat's eaten Fudge!"

Carole ran upstairs, followed by Bob with Sarah in his arms. Neil pounded up behind and caught up with his parents in the doorway of Sarah's bedroom. On the table by the window, the hamster cage was empty. The door was hanging open.

On the bed Tai-Lu the Siamese cat was sprawled on her side. Her jewel-like eyes were slits. She looked full and happy. Neil was sure she was smiling.

Bob sat on the bed and pulled Sarah onto his knee. Carole knelt down beside them. Neil watched, feeling helpless, and wondering what else could go wrong. Emily, white-faced but no longer crying, had arrived as well, and even Sam, disturbed by all the noise, had

followed them up the stairs.

Sarah's face was buried in her father's shoulder.

"Don't cry, love," Carole said soothingly. "Tell me what happened."

"The cat ate Fudge."

"But how – were you playing with him? Did you have him out of the cage?"

"Yes – but I put him back. I did, Mummy."

Neil guessed that Sarah hadn't fastened the cage door properly. It wasn't the first time that Fudge had made a dash for freedom, but they had always managed to catch him quite easily. Sarah would be even more upset if she thought it was her fault.

"I knew this would happen," Carole said angrily.

"Don't cry, pet," Bob said, stroking Sarah's tangled hair. "You can have another hamster." Sarah looked up, her face flushed and tearful.

"Don't want another hamster. I want Fudge."

Fudge was special. According to Sarah, he was the best, the most intelligent, the friendliest hamster in the whole world. Neil knew she wouldn't want another.

As he stood there, Neil found himself

watching Sam. The Border collie was snuffling at the gap between Sarah's wardrobe and the skirting board.

"Sam? What's up, boy?" Sam looked up at him, and whined softly.

"It looks as if he's found a . . . mouse?" Emily's eyes widened suddenly.

Neil grinned. "Get that cat out of here."

Emily scooped up Tai-Lu and went out, shutting the door behind her.

Neil grabbed Sam's collar and tried to peer behind the wardrobe. He couldn't see anything, and all he could hear were Sarah's sobs.

"Squirt, shut up a minute," he said.

"Neil . . ." Carole began. She looked up, saw what Neil was doing, and came over to him. "Neil, do you think—"

"I don't know. But Sam's found something. Can you go round the other side, Mum."

Carole went to the other side of the wardrobe and gave it a shove. There was a scrabbling noise. A small, golden head poked out of the gap. Sam gave a single, excited bark. Carole bashed the wardrobe again and Neil caught Fudge neatly with one hand as he popped out onto the carpet.

Sarah was staring, hiccuping as she tried to hold her sobs back. She didn't start to smile until Neil put the quivering golden body into her cupped hands.

"Oh, Neil . . . thank you!" said Sarah.

Neil flushed with embarrassment. "I didn't find him. It was Sam."

Sarah scrambled off her father's knee and tried to hug Sam and Fudge at the same time.

"Let's put him back in the cage," Carole said.

Happily, Sarah did as she was told.

"I'm going to make Sam a medal," she said. "And I'll paint a big picture of him and Fudge."

Carole followed the rest of the family into the kitchen.

"I knew there'd be trouble with that creature in the house," she said.

"That's not fair," Emily protested. She spooned cat food into a bowl, and Tai-Lu weaved round her ankles, purring loudly. "Tai-Lu just happened to be in Sarah's room at the wrong time. She hadn't done anything to Fudge." She waved the spoon. "The cat is innocent!"

"Of course!" said Neil, suddenly.

Emily's eyes met his. She stood frozen, the

bowl of cat food forgotten in her hands. Each knew what the other was thinking.

"Skye's innocent as well," Neil said. "She just happened to be in that field at the wrong time."

"And we've got to prove it, Neil!"

Tai-Lu let out an indignant, high-pitched howling, and Emily hastily put the bowl down in front of her. Sam looked on enviously, but he knew better than to get too close.

"Let's make a plan," Emily said.

She grabbed a pencil and paper and sat down at the kitchen table. Neil sat opposite. He felt better already.

"We know Skye didn't kill that sheep, right?" he began. "So there must be another dog who did. We have to find it."

"I suppose we could ask at all the other cottages in Rookery Lane. Find out if anyone saw anything." Emily made a careful note of what Neil said, and sat sucking her pencil. "It's happened three times now . . . And it's bound to be the same dog . . . Maybe Skye has an alibi for the two previous attacks."

Neil shook his head. "She was living up the lane with Mr Bradshaw then."

"But we don't know what she was doing. If

we knew exactly when the sheep were killed, we might be able to find out where Skye was at the time."

"And how do we find out?" Neil asked. "Do you fancy going to ask Mr Milton?"

"If we have to. But I've got a better idea!" Emily dropped the pencil and excitedly ran her hands through her hair. "Maybe it got into the paper. Jake Fielding is coming on Monday to take pictures of Bundle. He might be able to tell us."

"And have this whole horrible mess splashed all over the *Compton News*?" Carole said, banging a pan on the cooker. "No thank you. Not if we can help it."

"Jake wouldn't do that," Emily said.

"It's his job, Emily. If you want to know what's in the paper, why don't you try reading it?"

Neil shrugged and went to fetch the latest issue of the *Compton News* from the sitting room. He and Emily divided it up and settled down at opposite sides of the table. Neil was hoping they would not have to go looking for back issues, but he hadn't expected Emily's sudden cry of "Yes!" after only a couple of minutes.

"Show me," he said.

Emily turned the paper round so Neil could see. She pointed to a small article at the bottom of an inside page, headlined DANGEROUS DOG AT LARGE. Neil read it aloud:

"Police were called to a Compton farm last Saturday after complaints that a dog had attacked and killed two sheep. Farmer Geoffrey Milton, 48, of Causeway Farm, stated that he had found the sheep dead when he checked the field in the late afternoon. Police examined the area but no arrest has yet been made. This latest attack was the second time sheep at Causeway Farm had been killed in as many weeks; there was a similar occurrence the previous Saturday."

"That's it!" Emily's eyes shone. "That's just what we want to know."

"Last Saturday," Neil said. "And the weekend before. How can we find out what Skye was doing then?"

"Ask Mr Bradshaw," Emily said, and frowned. "No, we can't do that."

"You're right. We can't ask Mr Bradshaw anything," Neil said. "Not without telling him about Skye. And I don't know how to do that."

"Don't rush into anything," Carole said. She was now peeling potatoes at the sink. "Mr Bradshaw is an old man, and he hasn't been well."

"If we can get this cleared up quickly," Neil said, "we might not have to tell him at all."

But they still had to find out where Skye had been on the two other occasions when sheep were killed. Neil was trying to think it through when his father came into the kitchen.

Neil showed him the report they had found in the *News*.

"If this other dog has killed three times already, it might try again," he said excitedly. "Maybe we can be there when it does!"

"Aren't you forgetting a few minor details?" his mother said. "Like school, for example? Besides, if the dog kills again when Skye's locked up, won't that be just as good?"

"Maybe," Neil said. "But proving that the other dog did it would be better."

"Mum, don't you want to help Skye?" Emily said.

Carole sighed and came to sit with them at the table.

"Yes, of course I do. But look – you two might have got yourselves shot, we've had the police in the house, and your father could be prosecuted. I don't want any more trouble."

"But that means we've got to do it for Dad's sake as well," Neil said.

"Oh, go on then," Carole said. "But don't do anything without asking one of us first. Is that clear?"

While supper was cooking, Neil slipped out and cycled down the road to his friend Chris Wilson's house. He went to Meadowbank School with Neil, and although he lived for football while Neil lived for dogs, the two boys were good friends. They even looked alike, with the same wiry build and the same untidy brown hair.

Neil found Chris in his bedroom. The walls were plastered with football posters. Neil flopped down onto the bed. "Chris, I need a word."

"OK. Shoot."

Neil could have done without the mention of shooting.

"Can I borrow your camera?" he asked.

Chris had a really good camera, with a zoom lens and all the attachments. It was just what Neil needed for the plan he had in mind.

"Sure," Chris said. "What do you want it for?"

Neil explained about Skye, and the danger she was in, and what might happen to his father. By the time he had finished, Chris was sitting up, bright-eyed.

"Cool!" he said. "You're gonna stake out the field, right?"

"Right. Well, tomorrow and after school next week, anyway. And if anything happens, I'll be able to take pictures as evidence. I want to get an early start, so can you show me how to use the camera?"

"I'll do better than that," Chris said. "I'll come with you."

Chapter Eight

Very early the next morning, Neil and Chris were on their bikes heading for Rookery Lane with Sam bounding along beside them. Emily had wanted to go too, but preferred to stop at King Street and help her parents with the large number of owners who were leaving and collecting their dogs.

Neil and Chris were soon looking over the drystone wall into Geoffrey Milton's field. Sam put his paws up on the wall and looked too.

The sheep were grazing peacefully. There was no sign of trouble, and no sign of the farmer and his dog. Neil began to realize that keeping watch wasn't going to be as simple as he had thought at first. It was a big field, and most of it was out of sight because of the hill.

"Do we just sit here?" Chris said. He sounded less enthusiastic than he had the night before. "What if it rains?"

"Let's walk up the lane," Neil said.

Carole Parker had forbidden him to go asking from door to door about Skye, but she hadn't said anything about stopping to have a chat with anybody who happened to be out in their garden. Or about having a good look at each cottage for signs that a dog lived there.

As Neil and Chris passed a cottage near the middle of the row, the door opened and a woman came out with a beagle on a lead. Neil paused, and as the woman opened her garden gate the beagle leapt up at him, her white tail waving happily.

"Down, Sukie!" her owner said. "I'm sorry," she continued, speaking to Neil. "She's a bit excitable."

The beagle was standing still now, looking up at Neil with liquid eyes. Neil squatted down and let her smell his fingers.

"You're an old softy, you are," he said, admiring her tan and white coat and stroking her long, silky ears.

"She is, isn't she?"

"Are there many dogs round here?" Neil asked.

The woman gave him a funny look, as if she couldn't see the point of the question, but she answered him.

"No, not really. There used to be a collie up at the top of the lane – a beautiful dog – but Mr Bradshaw got too old to cope on his own and moved away."

She smiled at Neil and persuaded Sukie,

who was now touching noses with Sam, to go trotting after her down the lane. Neil watched them go. That settled it. There were no suspects in Rookery Lane. That soppy beagle would fly more easily than she could kill sheep.

At the top of the lane, Neil and Chris noticed a battered van parked outside number 11. The cottage door stood open, and sounds of movement came from inside. As the boys watched, a young woman came out, took a bundle of pink and purple cushions from the back of the van, and went back in.

"The new people are moving in," Neil said.

They passed the van, leaving their bikes propped against the wall, and went to lean on the five-bar gate at the end of the lane. Chris started to fiddle with his camera. Neil watched him for a few minutes, until a voice behind him called, "Hello!"

It was the young woman from the cottage. She was small and slim, with long fair hair, and she wore jeans and a baggy pink shirt.

"Hello," Neil said.

"Do you know where we can get milk at this time on a Sunday?"

"There's a garage on the Compton Road."

"Oh, good." The young woman smiled. "I knew I'd forget something! Can you give me directions? We're new to Compton."

Chris pushed the camera into Neil's hands. "If you see anything, press that." Chris began to explain the best route she should take.

The woman closed the back of the van and then shouted to someone unseen in the cottage. "I'm going to get some milk!" She climbed into the driving seat and the van jolted off down the lane.

Neil examined the camera, and then stared out into the field. The sheep were still chewing the grass peacefully, and nothing was happening. *What a waste of time*, he thought.

Suddenly, they heard footsteps, and both turned to see a tall, dark-haired man with a neat beard.

"Hi," he said, leaning on the gate beside Neil. "We're just moving in. Do you live near here?"

"Yes, my mum and dad run King Street Kennels. I'm Neil Parker. This is Chris."

"Mark Ford." The man held out his hand and Neil and Chris both shook it. "That's my wife Alison in the van. Nice camera," he added.

"It's mine," said Chris.

"I wouldn't have thought there's much to photograph up here."

Neil wasn't sure how it happened, but they found themselves telling Mark the whole story – all about Skye and Mr Bradshaw and the dead sheep. Alison came back before they'd finished and Neil had to explain it all over again for her.

"That's terrible!" she said when Neil had described Skye being taken away. "Poor dog! We've got to do something."

"Could you?" Neil said hopefully.

Mark scratched his beard.

"Well, we can help you keep watch," he said. "Not all day and night, but we can keep our eyes open. Give us your phone number, and we'll let you know if there's any more trouble."

"Thanks!" Neil said.

"And for now," Alison suggested, bending down to fondle Sam, "why don't you come indoors? You'll see a lot more from our top floor windows than you will standing down here."

"But we'll be in the way . . ." Neil said.

"Doesn't matter," said Mark. "It's chaos in there anyway."

"I know," Chris said. "We can help you out – well, one of us can, while the other one keeps watch."

"You're on." Mark straightened up and rubbed his hands. "Why are we all standing here, then?"

For the rest of the day Neil and Chris stayed in the cottage. They took it in turns – one watched in the bedroom while the other helped Mark and Alison get organized. But by the time it started to get dark, they were still no closer to finding the dog that had really attacked the sheep.

"Cheer up," Mark said, as the boys said goodbye. "You can't expect to strike lucky the first day. Come again whenever you want."

"And look," Alison said, "this is Skye's basket, isn't it, and her blanket and rubber bone? They got left behind. Do you want them?"

"We could keep them for her," Neil said.

"We'll drop them round to the kennels in the van," Alison promised. "She'll be back in no time, you'll see."

*

Neil was not sure about that. He felt even less sure next morning, when he had to go to school. It was hard to concentrate on work with the threat to Skye looming over him.

As soon as Neil got home from school, Emily dragged him out to tidy up the rescue centre. "Jake Fielding's coming at five o'clock to take pictures of Bundle. I want everything to look right."

Seeing Skye's empty pen made Neil feel depressed. Alison had brought in her dog basket during the day and it looked slightly less bare, but the beautiful collie's absence was all the more noticeable.

Bundle leapt up to the wire to welcome them, his tail wagging vigorously. The sight of the pink pooch made him more cheerful. He slipped Bundle a dog treat.

"Good boy," Emily said. "We're going to find you a wonderful owner, just you wait and see. Somebody really nice."

"I dunno," said Neil. "Anybody who would want a pink dog would have to be pretty peculiar. And colour-blind."

Before Emily could reply Bob Parker came into the rescue centre, along with Jake Fielding, the photographer from the *Compton*

News. He was a tall young man with his hair in a ponytail. The pockets of his denim jacket were stuffed with spare lenses and film.

He stopped in front of Bundle's pen, and gazed at the dog in silence for a minute.

"You see a lot in this job," he said at last, "but I've never seen a pink mutt before. You need shades to look at him."

"Don't laugh," Neil pleaded.

Jake was grinning and shaking his head, as if he didn't really believe what he was seeing.

"Pity the *News* is only black and white," he said. "He could fill a colour supplement all by himself." He began adjusting the settings on his camera. "Right, Emily, can we have him out here."

Emily went into the pen and Bundle bounced excitedly around her.

"Down, boy!" she said. "If you don't keep still, you can't have your picture taken."

Bundle trotted after her out of the pen and sat in front of Jake, looking up with his tongue hanging out and one ear cocked. Jake laughed.

"Look at him, mugging for the camera! Bags of personality – just what our readers want.

He's going to come fizzing off the page."

Jake took several photographs of Bundle from lots of different angles – some alone, some with Emily cuddling him. Bundle enjoyed every minute of it.

When Jake had finished, and was putting away the camera and labelling the film, he said, "My aunt is looking for somewhere to board her dog. I recommended you."

"Thanks," Bob said, smiling. "Tell me her name, and I'll see she gets five-star treatment."

"Mary Fielding. The dog's a Jack Russell called Pooch." Jake bent over to rumple

Bundle's ears. "Stupid name, but a very intelligent dog. Do you know, every Friday afternoon my aunt goes shopping, and every Friday morning without fail Pooch brings her the shopping bag."

"Dogs pick up signals from their owners," Bob pointed out. "Left to themselves, they wouldn't know what day it is."

He moved towards the door, showing Jake out.

"Don't you worry, boy," he said, looking at Bundle. "Everything's going to be fine."

When his father had left with Jake, Neil stared after them thoughtfully. Something they said had just clicked in his mind and he was trying to work out why. Emily put Bundle back in his pen and opened the door to the outer run.

"What's the matter with you?" she asked.

"Emily . . ." Neil was speaking slowly. "What happened to that newspaper report about the dangerous dog?"

"It's in the kitchen. Why?"

"Come on!"

Emily had cut out the report and pinned it to the kitchen noticeboard alongside her mother's shopping list. Excitement surged through Neil as he read aloud from the article. He was sure he was onto something.

"Police were called to a Compton Farm last Saturday . . . This latest attack was the second time sheep at Causeway Farm had been killed in as many weeks; there was a similar occurrence the previous Saturday . . .

"Emily, you heard what Dad just said. Left to themselves, dogs don't know what day it is. But all three attacks have happened on a Saturday. This dog seems to be attacking Mr Milton's sheep at the same time every week!"

Emily frowned, trying to puzzle it out

"It could only do that . . ."

". . . If somebody took it there," Neil finished the sentence for her.

"Deliberately?" asked Emily.

Brother and sister stared at each other.

"Well," Neil said, "there's only one way to find out. We'll have to be there next Saturday."

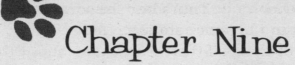

Chapter Nine

The rest of the week seemed to last for ever. On the Wednesday evening, Tom Dewhurst rang up from The Grange. Mr Bradshaw had been asking when Skye could come and see him again.

Faced with deciding whether or not to tell Tom what had happened to Skye, Neil found that he couldn't bring himself to admit the truth. He stalled Tom with wild excuses. He even said that he had too much homework! Tom was puzzled, but he agreed to get in touch again nearer the weekend. Neil knew that he suspected something was wrong.

When Bob Parker picked up Neil and Emily

after school on Thursday, he drove them straight to the police station.

"I want to ask if there's any news about the court case," he explained. "And they might let us see Skye."

Sergeant Moorhead was not in the station when the Parkers arrived. The desk sergeant, a newcomer who didn't know the Parkers, was friendly but could not tell them anything new.

"Your case will come up when there's space in the magistrate's list," he told Bob. "You'll be informed in good time."

"And what about Skye?" Neil asked anxiously. "Is she all right?" The desk sergeant smiled.

"She's fine. Do you want to pay her a visit?"

He called a young constable who took the Parkers to the back of the police station, where there were pens for stray dogs.

Skye was lying in the nearest pen, her nose on her paws, her eyes half shut. She raised her head when Neil said her name, and let out a soft whine.

"She's pining," Emily said.

"Here, Skye." Neil offered her a dog treat through the wire, and after a moment she padded up and took it. "Good dog," Neil said. "Don't you worry. We'll soon have you out of here." But he could not help wondering if he would be able to keep his promise.

Saturday was overcast, and it was threatening to rain when Neil, Emily and Chris pushed their bikes up Rookery Lane. This time, Neil had left Sam at home. He was worried that with a savage dog around his beloved Border collie might get hurt.

Outside number 11 Mark was stripping paint from the woodwork with a blowlamp.

"Hi," he said. "We've been expecting you. Go in and see Alison."

Alison was baking in the kitchen. Warm, delicious smells wafted towards them, and each of the three took a piece of hot spice-bread up to the lookout on the top floor.

Here, Neil told Chris about his theory that someone was letting a dog loose in the field at the same time every Saturday afternoon.

"You mean to say that somebody is deliberately setting his dog on Geoffrey Milton's sheep?" Chris said. "Who would do a thing like that? Somebody with a grudge against sheep?"

"Or somebody who doesn't like Geoffrey Milton," Neil said.

"I can't believe it." Chris took his camera out of its cover and started to screw in a long, sophisticated-looking lens. "But just in case you're right, I'll be ready."

Not long after lunch, Mark went off in the van to buy paint. Chris was downstairs with Alison when a sudden movement in the field caught Neil's eye. The sheep were scattering. A black shape darted back and forth among them.

"This is it!" Neil roared.

He clattered down the uncarpeted stairs, Emily behind him.

"Chris!" he yelled. "Fetch the camera! Quick!"

He had a brief glimpse of Alison's astonished face as he dashed out of the front door.

Outside, sheep were running across the brow of the hill. Neil could hear their frantic, terrified bleating. He leapt over the five-bar gate, racing ahead. Emily followed, then Chris clambered over it more slowly clutching the camera.

When Neil came to the top of the rise, he

could see the rest of the field spread out before him, sloping down to another drystone wall and a road beyond where a van was parked.

Closer, among the frightened sheep, a large black dog was bounding to and fro, barking aggressively. Flecks of foam glistened around its gaping jaws. Beyond it was a man, tall and thickset, shouting to urge the dog on, and waving a heavy, gnarled stick.

Neil swallowed his fears and started to run down the slope towards the man. "Call your dog off!" he shouted.

The man saw him and shouted something

back, which Neil did not catch because of the dog's brutal bark and the panic-stricken bleating of the sheep. Neil skidded to a halt directly in front of the man and stared up at him.

"Call him off! He'll kill the sheep!"

"Aye, and a good job, too. That Milton—"

He broke off, staring past Neil. At the top of the slope stood Emily and Chris. Chris had raised his camera, and was taking photographs one after another, as fast as he could.

The man pushed Neil away and surged up the slope towards Chris, shouting, "I'll smash that camera, you little . . ."

Neil ran after him. "Chris!"

Chris took one last photograph and then darted aside, sprinting around the man and on down the hill. The man changed direction but he was heavy, clumsy on his feet, and no match for Chris who trained on the football field several times a week. Even with the awkward camera to slow him down, he soon started to pull ahead.

He was pounding down the slope towards the road. Once he had outdistanced the man, Neil saw him stop and take a photograph of the van. The man was getting closer, lumbering towards him.

"Chris!" Neil shouted. "That's enough! Quick! Get back to the cottage!"

Chris ran down to the wall by the van and leant over. For a minute Neil was not sure what he was doing. Then he realized he must be photographing the number plate.

Well done, Chris, he thought. *You're brilliant!*

Suddenly, in front of him, Neil caught sight of the dog. It pounced on one of the sheep and its jaws locked firmly around the animal's throat. The barking became a low snarling noise. The sheep struggled bravely, then fell onto its back, its legs jerking frantically in the air.

Neil hesitated, and Emily started to run down the slope, waving her arms to attract the man's attention.

"Get off!" she cried. "Leave it alone!"

"Em! No!"

Neil flung himself towards her and managed to grab her before she reached the dog.

She fought against him. "Don't! That poor sheep . . ."

"Em, it's too late. It's already dead!"

As Neil held Emily back, he heard the roar of an engine. At first he thought it must be the van. Then he saw a Land Rover bouncing across the field towards them. Disturbed, the dog looked up and released his killer grip on the sheep.

Geoffrey Milton was at the wheel of the Land Rover. It swept past. The black dog chased it, barking.

Spraying mud, the farmer slammed to a halt at the bottom of the field where the dog's owner was still trying to catch up with Chris. When he saw Geoffrey Milton he started to run towards his van.

The farmer chased him, and brought him down with a rugby tackle just before he reached the wall. Neil couldn't help cheering.

While the two men wrestled on the ground, Chris was darting around them, taking photographs. Neil could see he was loving the drama of the situation.

"Come on," he said to Emily.

They started to run down the slope, but before they reached the two struggling men they heard the sound of a police siren, faint at first but growing rapidly louder. A police car pulled up at the roadside and Sergeant

Moorhead got out, followed by a constable.

Neil and Emily slowed down, panting, and walked the last few metres to the group by the wall. Geoffrey Milton pulled the other man to his feet. Neither of them had realized the police had arrived.

"Frank Jarvis!" the farmer spat. His broad face was red with fury. "I told you to keep off my land."

The other man struggled, but Geoffrey Milton had him firmly in an armlock.

"Thought you could do as you like, did you, Milton?" he snarled back. "Thought you could sack me and get away with it?"

Geoffrey Milton made a disgusted noise. Catching sight of Sergeant Moorhead, who had climbed the wall and had a pair of handcuffs ready, he thrust Jarvis towards him.

"Arrest this man, Sergeant," he said. "His name's Frank Jarvis. He used to work for me until a few weeks ago, but I sacked him for ill-treating one of my dogs. If this brute of a dog is a killer – he's responsible."

"You told us about that!" Neil exclaimed. "You told us, and I never thought . . ."

Geoffrey Milton turned and saw him.

"I'm sorry, lad," he said. "You were right

about Skye. I jumped to the wrong conclusion. That poor collie had nothing to do with it."

Sergeant Moorhead quickly snapped the handcuffs on Jarvis's wrists, and gave him the official caution. A constable hustled the man into the back of the police car.

The black dog was barking uncontrollably, standing stiff-legged a few metres away from the scene of its owner's arrest. Neil got a proper look at it for the first time. It was a big dog, and mostly black with a few tan markings: a mongrel, Neil guessed, with a lot of Dobermann in it.

"Constable," Sergeant Moorhead said, "we need to get a muzzle on that animal."

"Er . . . yes, sir."

The two policemen looked at each other. Neil could see that neither of them fancied trying to handle the black dog. He couldn't blame them. The dog was dangerous; if what Geoffrey Milton said was true, its owner had deliberately trained it to be aggressive. Neil couldn't imagine how anyone could treat a dog like that.

"Do you want me to have a try, Sergeant?" the farmer said. Sergeant Moorhead shook his head.

"It's our responsibility, sir."

"It's my land."

Just then the King Street Kennels Range Rover swept round the corner and joined the vans parked beside the road. Bob Parker leapt out of the driver's seat, and Alison appeared from the other side.

"Neil! Emily! Are you all right?" their father said.

"Fine, Dad," said Neil.

"I thought you were watching from the lane, not running around in the field."

Sergeant Moorhead nodded to Bob, and brought him up to date with what was happening. Alison sat on the wall.

"Was it you who rang the police?" Neil asked.

"Yes." Alison brushed wisps of fair hair out of her eyes. "And the farmer. And your parents. And then I waited for your father to arrive so I could show him where you were." She let out a sigh of relief. "I was scared stiff."

Bob Parker was climbing over the wall into the field.

"Have you got a muzzle?" he asked. The constable went to fetch one from the van. Sergeant Moorhead started to protest.

"This is my job, Sergeant," Bob said. He grinned. "You know about villains, but I know about dogs." He jerked his head at Neil and the others. "You three. Over the wall."

Bob Parker didn't often use that tone of voice, but when he did, no one argued. When everybody, except for the sergeant and Geoffrey Milton, was safely out of the field, Bob walked slowly towards the dog.

A couple of metres in front of it he stopped. He stood with his arms at his sides, offering nothing for the dog to grab if it sprang at him. He spoke calmly.

"Quiet, boy. Sit."

The dog stayed standing, but its barking stopped. Instead it let out a low growl from deep inside its throat. Neil thought that sounded even nastier. He hadn't let himself be afraid when he was in the field with the dog; now he was frightened, but he knew if anyone could bring it under control, it was his father.

"Sit," Bob said quietly and firmly.

That note of command in Bob Parker's voice was not disobeyed by many dogs and this vicious creature was no exception. It sat, though it still kept up its menacing low growl. Neil felt Emily gripping his arm tightly. He realized he had forgotten to keep breathing.

Bob took a pace forward. The dog stayed still.

"Quiet, boy," Bob said. "That's fine. Just fine."

Still speaking in the same reassuring tones, he went right up to the dog and bent over to fit on the muzzle. The dog leapt to its feet again, but Bob held the muzzle in place as it fought to free itself. He kept his movements slow and deliberate, and never stopped talking. He fastened the muzzle and clipped on the lead. Neil let out his breath and found that he was shaking.

"Wow!" Chris said.

Geoffrey Milton grabbed Bob's hand and shook it vigorously. Sergeant Moorhead was about to join him when Emily put a hand on his arm.

"Please, sergeant," she said, "can we have our dog back now?"

Chapter Ten

ob Parker drove home, leaving Neil, Emily and Chris to follow on their bikes. When Neil and Emily cycled through the gates of King Street Kennels, Neil saw a familiar car parked in the drive.

Mrs Downes, the owner of Ming and Tai-Lu, was standing beside it, talking to Carole. Mrs Downes looked much more suntanned than she had the week before, and much more embarrassed.

". . . and if you'd been honest with me," his mother was saying, "instead of palming off the cat on us when—"

"Now look here . . ." A tall dark-haired man,

whom Neil supposed was Mr Downes, tried to interrupt.

"No, *you* look. I'd have been quite willing to help out in an emergency, but I don't like to be taken advantage of. Emily, go and put *that creature* in its pet carrier."

Emily ran up the steps and disappeared into the house.

"I'm really sorry," Mrs Downes said. "We had to get away, and we couldn't think what else to do. If you want an extra fee . . ."

"It's not a question of money," Carole said. "It's a question of the welfare of your pets, which we seem to care about rather more than you do."

While she was speaking, Bob Parker appeared through the side gate with Ming in his carrier and Sam trotting along beside him.

"On the other hand," he added, "if you want to make a donation to the rescue centre, we wouldn't say no."

Looking sulky, Mr Downes took out his chequebook and rested it on the bonnet of the car to write a cheque, which he then gave to Carole. Mrs Downes repeated her apologies.

Emily came out with Tai-Lu. Of them all, Neil thought, she was the only one sorry to see the Siamese cat go. Even Sam gave an approving bark as the cat's carrier was placed in the back of the car.

As Mr and Mrs Downes drove away, a police dog van passed them in the entrance and drew up in the drive. Sergeant Moorhead got out, and opened the back door.

"Skye!" Emily cried when she saw the dog leap out onto the ground. "Oh, Skye, you're home!"

The rough collie had got all her bounce back. She leapt up at Neil and Emily, until Neil said firmly, "Sit!"

Neil laughed. It was good to have her back.

"You were right all along," Sergeant Moorhead said. "She's lively, but she's gentle. She's been no trouble." He turned to Bob. "You can stop worrying now, Mr Parker. As far as you're concerned, it's all over."

"I can't say I'm sorry," Bob said.

"Jarvis will be up before the magistrate in a few days," Sergeant Moorhead told them. "He's admitted everything. Mind you, he hadn't much choice, not with your kids as witnesses, and their young friend's roll of film."

"And it was all because Mr Milton sacked him?" Neil asked.

"That's right. Revenge. He used to work for Geoffrey Milton, but the farmer ordered him off his land when he found him ill-treating one of his sheepdogs. Jarvis found another job delivering for an animal feed firm, and his route took him past that field every Saturday afternoon. That's when he was setting the dog on the sheep."

"We knew there was some reason for the pattern!" Neil said.

"Well spotted," said the sergeant. "It was just Skye's bad luck that she came along while the sheep was lying dead."

"At least it's all right now," Emily said, hugging Skye's head.

"And what's going to happen to the dog?" Neil asked.

"The magistrate will make an order," Sergeant Moorhead told him. "Either to have it controlled, or put down."

"It can't be retrained?" asked Neil.

Bob Parker shook his head slowly.

"I doubt it, Neil. It's been mistreated. It's used to killing now."

Neil knew that his father was right.

They said goodbye to Sergeant Moorhead and went back into the house. But that wasn't the end, Neil thought to himself. Skye was safe, and it probably wouldn't be much trouble to find her a new owner. But the original problem still remained; Skye and Mr Bradshaw were going to be parted for ever.

Sergeant Moorhead was not the last visitor to the kennels that evening. Carole was preparing supper when Mark and Alison Ford drove up in their old van. Neil answered the door.

"We had to come and find out whether everything's all right," Mark said. "Especially when I missed all the fun. Have you got Skye back?"

"Yes," Neil said. "She's back in her pen, and she was really pleased to find her basket. Would you like to see her?"

"Yes, please," said Alison. "And we'd like to see the pink dog, too." She spread out the copy of the *Compton News* she was clutching, and showed Neil a picture of Bundle. "No one's claimed him yet, have they?"

"Not yet," Neil said, grinning.

He showed Mark and Alison the way round the back of the house and across the courtyard to the rescue centre. He had been hoping that Mark and Alison might take Skye, so she could at least go back to her old home, if not to her owner. But now it looked as if they might give a home to Bundle instead.

Inside the rescue centre, Skye padded up to them with a look of friendly interest.

"She's a beauty," Mark said admiringly.

But Alison was looking in the pen across the way.

"Oh, Mark, he's here!" Bundle had come over to see what was going on. "Look, he's gorgeous. However could they do that to him?"

Neil unfastened the door of the pen and Alison went inside. She knew just how to approach Bundle, squatting down and holding

114

out a hand to him, not startling him with quick movements or by going too close too soon. Bundle gave her hand a good sniff, and then lifted one paw to lay it on her knee, while he gazed appealingly up into her face.

"Crikey!" Mark said. "He'd charm the feathers off the birds!"

Alison looked up at him, bright-eyed.

"Mark, could we . . .? You know we said we'd get a dog, once we were settled. And he's so beautiful."

"He's going to be big." Neil felt he had to warn her. "And he's – well, he's pink."

"That'll soon grow out," Alison said. "And I like big dogs. Mark, what do you think?"

Mark sighed, pretending to sound resigned, but he was looking just as happy as his wife.

"Well, if you really want him . . ."

"Can we take him now?" Alison begged.

Neil's face broke into a wide grin.

Tom Dewhurst called from The Grange the next day. Neil gave Skye another thorough grooming and in the afternoon Bob Parker drove him and Emily and Skye out to the country house. Matron had invited them to come to tea, and to bring Sam and Skye. Sarah went along as well, because she had made such a fuss about being left out.

Bob dropped them off at the gates of The Grange, and Neil and Emily led the dogs, both on their leads, up the drive. Sarah skipped alongside, singing maddeningly.

"Shut up, Squirt," Neil said. "Behave yourself."

"Shut up yourself," she retorted.

At least, Neil thought, she'd stopped worshipping him for saving Fudge. That had felt very uncomfortable.

They followed the path through the shrubbery round the side of the house, and Tom met them by the kitchen door as before. But this time they weren't sneaking in; this time they were invited guests.

It was a sunny day and the residents of The Grange were sitting on the terrace at the back of the house. As Neil and the others drew closer he could see some other people. To his surprise, Marjorie Foster was sitting beside her father, looking much more relaxed and happy than she had done that night in Mike Turner's surgery.

Another person Neil had not expected to see was Dr Harvey, sprawled in a chair next to Matron, at the other end of the terrace. He waved cheerfully at Neil; they knew each other well because Alex Harvey brought his dogs, Finn and Sandy, to Bob Parker's obedience classes.

Neil glanced anxiously at Tom. "What's up?"

Tom gave him a gleeful nod. He was tense with excitement; his wiry hair looked as if it was going to spring off his head. "Wait and see."

Skye began to bark when she saw Mr Bradshaw and pulled towards him, but Neil was ready for her this time and he made her walk across the lawn and up the steps to sit beside the old man. Mr Bradshaw laid a hand on her head.

"Eh, lass," he said. "You're looking grand."

Matron got up and shook Neil, Emily and Sarah by the hand. One of the staff brought out the tea trolley and handed round tea and cake. Sam was being thoroughly petted, and Sarah was making friends with half a dozen old ladies at once.

Matron led Neil, Emily and Tom over to Dr Harvey. "Now," she said, "this isn't just an ordinary invitation."

"I thought as much," Neil said, and then wondered if that sounded rude.

Matron smiled. "I think Dr Harvey ought to be the person who tells you what we're planning."

Dr Harvey put his cup of tea to one side.

"Now, you know that up to now The Grange has had a no pets policy."

At the words "up to now" Neil drew in a deep breath and exchanged a look with Emily. Alex Harvey was also smiling.

"However," he went on, stroking his beard, "recent research shows that old people are much happier, have much more of an interest in life, and sometimes live longer, if they're in close contact with a pet. So Matron has decided that for the good of the residents, The Grange should change its policy and have at least one official pet."

"And it's going to be Skye!" Tom couldn't keep quiet any longer. "I'll look after her and exercise her, but she'll still be Mr Bradshaw's dog."

"That's brilliant!" Emily said, punching the air.

Neil looked over at Mr Bradshaw. Skye was resting her muzzle on the old man's knee, and neither dog nor owner was paying any

attention to anyone else. Neil's throat felt tight.

"Are you pleased?" Tom said. "I've never had a dog – I don't know much about them. You'll have to tell me what to do."

Neil found his voice. "No, there's somebody better than me. Somebody who can tell you all about Skye."

He nodded at Mr Bradshaw. Seeing the look, Marjorie Foster got up and came over to the group.

"You've told him?" she said to Matron. She took a spare seat beside Neil. "Dr Harvey tells me that your father runs obedience classes?"

"That's right," Neil said. "He's the best."

"We all think it would be a good idea for Skye to come to the classes," Marjorie went on. "Or the old people might find her a bit of a handful. Tom will bring her, and I'll pay."

"Is that OK?" Tom asked.

"OK?" Neil said. "Sure it's OK. Just leave it to the Puppy Patrol!"

Puppy Patrol titles available from Macmillan Children's Books

The prices shown below are correct at the time of going to press. However, Macmillan Publishers reserve the right to show new retail prices on covers which may differ from those previously advertised.

1.	Teacher's Pet	Jenny Dale	£2.99
2.	Big Ben	Jenny Dale	£2.99
3.	Abandoned!	Jenny Dale	£2.99
4.	Double Trouble	Jenny Dale	£2.99
5.	Star Paws	Jenny Dale	£2.99
6.	Tug of Love	Jenny Dale	£2.99
7.	Saving Skye	Jenny Dale	£2.99
8.	Tuff's Luck	Jenny Dale	£2.99
9.	Red Alert	Jenny Dale	£2.99
10.	The Great Escape	Jenny Dale	£2.99

All Macmillan titles can be ordered at your local bookshop or are available by post from:

Book Service by Post
PO Box 29, Douglas, Isle of Man IM99 1BQ

Credit cards accepted. For details:
Telephone: 01624 675137
Fax: 01624 670923
E-mail: bookshop@enterprise.net

Free postage and packing in the UK.
Overseas customers: add £1 per book (paperback)
and £3 per book (hardback).